The Party

TED BLEW INTO my house one Saturday morning. He didn't even knock. I was eating cereal and, as usual, my father was busy in his study.

"Hello, birthday boy!" Ted bellowed. "Where are the raspberries?"

"Sorry," I said. "You have the wrong house. My birthday was last week."

"Oh!" He frowned, then smiled a smug smile. "I'm Ted and raspberries are my favouritest food. They help keep me pinkish-purply. Do you have any?"

He looked harmless enough, so I found him some raspberries and sat down to finish my cereal.

"So, what's next, birthday boy?" asked Ted.

I shrugged. Then I remembered
my birthday gifts.

"Wait. I'll be right back!" A minute later
I returned with Monopoly under one arm and
Twister under the other.

"Father gave me these for my birthday, but
we haven't had a chance to play them yet."

"Then let's party!" Ted boomed.

And so we did. We ate raspberry-cereal
and played Monopoly-Twister!

I knew that this would be the beginning
of a fantastic friendship.

When I told Father about Ted, he gave me one of his funny looks.

"An imaginary friend, huh? I had one of those, back when I was your age. Just try not to get into trouble."

A shave and a haircut

A FEW DAYS LATER, I asked Father to take us to the cinema.

Ted thought I should look my best. "First things first. Take your bath and I'll give you a shave and a haircut."

"But kids my age don't shave."

"Didn't you just have a birthday?" Ted asked.

"That's right!" Boy, Ted was a genius.

Once I was out of the tub, Ted lathered my face all over and gave me a shave. Then he glued bits of toilet paper to my face.

"What are these?" I asked.

"Tissue plugs," Ted answered. "They'll keep your beard from growing back."

"Oh." So that's why Father does it.

Then it was time for my haircut.

I grabbed a chair and sat in front of the mirror. Ted tied a towel around me and snippy-snap! I looked *fantastic!*

But Father didn't think so.

"How . . . how . . . how could you do this?!" he asked.

"Ted helped me. Don't you think he did a great job?"

"Son, Ted didn't do this. You did." Father then spent the next four hours explaining the difference between real and imaginary friends. And I ended up at the barber where I got the haircut Father picked out.

We never made it to the cinema.

The Masterpiece

"I DON'T THINK my father believes in you," I said to Ted after the haircut-thing.

"No?" Ted gasped. "He must. He has to!"

Still, I didn't think so, but I had an idea.

"Maybe we should paint him a picture of you," I suggested.

"Oooooo! We can do a BIG, HUMONGOUS, LIFE-SIZE picture of me. I bet that would show your father!"

"But what do we do it on?" I asked. I didn't have any paper that was as HUMONGOUS as Ted.

"The walls, silly. They're so blank and boring."

And, whishy-whoosh . . .

Father didn't think so. He couldn't believe how much of a mess I had made – by myself – in one afternoon. That's when I reminded him about Ted.

"I have had about enough of this 'Ted' character!" Father said. "Now go and clean yourself up. *You're* going to bed early while *I* clean up this disaster."

I don't think Father even *looked* at our picture.

Indoor Swimming

"WHEN DID YOUR father become such a stuffy-pants?" Ted asked me the following afternoon. "And what do adults do for fun, anyway?"

I started listing all the things my father didn't have time for anymore. When I got to swimming, Ted's eyes lit up like marshmallows.

"Let's make him a swimming pool!"

I wasn't sure if a pool was such a good idea, especially after the painting disaster and the haircut-thing. So I had a few questions: "How do we make a pool? Where do we get the water?" And the thing that I wondered about most: "Where are we going to put it?"

Ted had everything covered.

"It's easy," Ted explained. "We use the garden hose, bring it in through the window, and splishy-splosh! We could even put it in your father's study!"

An indoor swimming pool. We'd be the only house on the whole block to have an indoor swimming pool.

I held the hose.

Ted turned on the water.

"Father's going to love this!"

He didn't.

Father was beside himself. "I HAVE HAD ENOUGH! I FORBID YOU TO EVER PLAY WITH TED AGAIN! NO MORE TED! EVER!"

After we drained the house, Ted told me it was time for him to leave.

"But where will you go?" I asked.

"Back home," he replied, "to the old playground."

For the whole of the next day, all I could think about was Ted. I felt really sad and alone. So I packed up my Monopoly, my Twister, my cereal and some raspberries, and I ran away to live with him.

Father was still hopping mad, so he didn't even notice me slip out.

dear dad,
I went to go live with ted at the old play-ground. please don't worry.

The Old Playground

WHEN I FOUND TED, I explained why I had run away.

"Oh, don't blame your father," he said. "Sometimes, when people grow up, they forget how to have fun. Your father told me that when he was your age."

"My father?!"

"Yup. But to him I wasn't 'Ted.' I was 'Ned.' Boy, the times we had playing space pirates. In fact, your father buried his Atomic Blaster right here, under this slide."

"You knew my father, too?!" I was amazed.

Suddenly, there was a torch shining in my face.

"You shouldn't have run off like that! I was worried about you."

It was my father.

"You were?" I smiled.

"Of course I was. I'm your dad. Now come on, we're going home."

"But what about Ted?" I asked.

My dad stopped. "There is no Ted, son."

"But there is," I said. "You used to play space pirates together, except you called him 'Ned'. He even knows where you buried your Atomic Blaster."

Dad was stunned. "Ned? . . . My Atomic Blaster . . . Father had forbidden us to play. . . . I lost it . . . somewhere. . . ."

"It's okay, Dad. Ted says you buried it here, underneath the slide."

"He's right! I REMEMBER!"

We started digging.

And there it was, a bit rusty in places, but it still lit up Dad's face: The Atomic Blaster had been found!

Dad gave me a great big hug . . . then looked straight at Ted.

"Ned! It's so good to see my raspberry-loving pal again!" Dad grinned.

Then Dad looked at me. "Have I ever shown you how to play space pirates?"

"No." I grinned. "Then can we play Monopoly-Twister?"

So we all went home and played the best-ever game of space pirates-Monopoly-Twister!

The End

This book is a warm hug to my mom and pop. Thanks for all of your love, support, and encouragement in letting me be what I wanted to be. —Love, Punky

POCKET
BOOKS

This edition published in 2004 by Pocket Books,
an imprint of Simon & Schuster UK Ltd
Africa House, 64-78 Kingsway, London WC2B 6AH

Originally published in 2001 by Simon and Schuster Books for Young Readers,
an imprint of Simon & Schuster Children's Publishing Division, New York

Text and illustrations copyright © 2001 Tony DiTerlizzi

Tony (and Ted) would like to thank Angela (for letting Ted stay so long) and Pilly (for all of her input,
thanks also to Victoria, Chava, Anahid, Alyssa, and Kevin for putting it all together

Special thanks to Hasbro for the use of MONOPOLY® and TWISTER®. MONOPOLY® and TWISTER®
are trademarks of Hasbro, Inc. © 2001 Hasbro, Inc. All rights reserved. Used with permission

The right of Tony DiTerlizzi to be identified as the author and illustrator of this work
has been asserted by him in accordance with the Copyright, Designs and Patents Act, 1988

Book design by Anahid Hamparian
The text of this book is set in 20-point Lomba Book and Fontdinerdotcom
The illustrations are rendered in watercolour, gouache, and coloured pencil

A CIP catalogue record for this book is available from the British Library upon request

ISBN 0-743-48983-7
Printed in China
1 3 5 7 9 10 8 6 4 2